THIS BOOK is dedicated to you, the reader.

Special thanks to Jodi Reamer, Jill Santopolo, Lily May, Ellice Lee, "T," and Tom Booth. Thank you for making THIS BOOK!
—A. D.

For Taylor
—T. B.

PHILOMEL BOOKS
An imprint of Penguin Random House LLC, New York

First published in the United States of America by Philomel Books,
an imprint of Penguin Random House LLC, 2021

Text copyright © 2021 by Angela DiTerlizzi
Illustrations copyright © 2021 by Tom Booth

Philomel Books is a registered trademark of Penguin Random House LLC.

Visit us online at penguinrandomhouse.com.

Library of Congress Cataloging-in-Publication Data

Names: DiTerlizzi, Angela, author. | Booth, Tom, 1983—illustrator.
Title: Have you seen this book? / written by Angela DiTerlizzi ; illustrated by Tom Booth.
Description: New York : Philomel Books, an imprint of Penguin Random House LLC, 2021. | Audience: Ages 4–8. | Audience: Grades 2–3. | Summary: A boy's favorite book is missing, and he describes it to the reader in great detail, including all the changes he made to it (like hedgehogs covering the pictures of the scary monsters) until you realize his missing book in in your hands. Identifiers: LCCN 2021013385 | ISBN 9780593116845 (hardcover) | ISBN 9780593116852 (ebook) Subjects: LCSH: Books and reading—Juvenile fiction. | Lost articles—Juvenile fiction. | Humorous stories. | CYAC: Books and reading—Fiction. | Lost and found possessions—Fiction. | Humorous stories. | LCGFT: Humorous fiction. | Picture books. Classification: LCC PZ7.D629 Hav 2021 | DDC [E]—dc23 LC record available at https://lccn.loc.gov/2021013385

Manufactured in China

10 9 8 7 6 5 4 3 2 1

Edited by Jill Santopolo • Design by Ellice M. Lee
Text set in Kidprint MT Pro

Art done in graphite, Procreate, and Adobe Photoshop and Illustrator.

HAVE YOU SEEN THIS BOOK?

THE BOOK OF YORE

Written by
Angela DiTerlizzi

Illustrated by
Tom Booth

PHILOMEL

Have you seen this book?
It has a cover. The cover looks like this.
If you see a book with this cover, you'll
know it's mine.

Have you seen this book?

This book has everything—a princess, unicorns, a knight, a wizard, a troll, goblins, and the biggest dragon I've ever seen.

Along time ago, in the Kingdom of Yore, lived a princess, a wizard, a dragon, and more.

There was peace in the kingdom, until the day the Princess Verbena was stolen away.

Have you seen this book?

It has pages.

Yeah, I know all books have pages, but in my book the pages with the unicorns on them are folded at the corners, because unicorns are the coolest—even if the unicorns are having a meltdown because their favorite princess is missing. If you see a book with folded corners and unicorns, that's my book.

stinky gross

Three ~~putrid~~ goblins and a ~~hideous~~ troll snatched Princess Verbena while out out on patrol.

Have you seen this book?

My book has words. Words written by the author, like *putrid* and *hideous*. I hope the author doesn't mind that that I wrote some easier words, like *stinky* and *gross*. If you see the words *stinky* and *gross*, you'll know it's my book.

Have you seen this book?
My book has pictures. Tons of creepy pictures of stinky goblins with pointy teeth. I stuck hedgehog stickers on them because hedgehogs are not creepy or stinky. If you see a book with adorable hedgehog stickers, that's my book.

The goblins cackled.
The troll said with a snort,
"Welcome to your new home—
the Castle Wormwort!"

In that very moment,
a wizard appeared.
Oh, this was far worse
than the princess had feared.

Have you seen this book?

My book has a wizard in it, with a really, really, really, really, really long beard—and an eye patch—and he's missing a tooth.

There's no hedgehog stickers on this page, because it's not as creepy as the goblin page.

And also because I ran out of hedgehog stickers.

Have you seen this book?
In my book, the wizard wants to marry the princess. She doesn't look that excited. Probably because he's evil AND he doesn't even have a ring!
I drew one in my book. If you see a book with a drawing of a ring, you'll know it's my book.
SCOUT

Verbena shouted, "No! You can't make me stay!" He laughed at the princess and locked her away.

Have you seen this book? In my book, the princess won't marry the hairy, evil wizard, so he locks her away. That's OK. I tucked a key in the page so she could unlock the door and escape. If you see a shiny gold key tucked in a page with a hairy, evil wizard, you'll know it's my book.

Have you seen this book?

My book had a key in it, but I guess it didn't unlock the door. That's OK, because my book has something more powerful—a hamster named SUPERNIBBLES. He has come to save the day! If you've seen SUPERNIBBLES, you've seen my book.

In the tallest tower,
the princess would wait
for a knight to arrive
and change her ill fate.

Have you seen this *book*?
Now, there's good news and there's *bad* news. The good news is that the knight and the princess escaped the evil wizard. The *bad* news is SUPERNIBBLES left because they didn't need his help. I really miss SUPERNIBBLES. So, I wrote a note to tell him that. If you've seen that note, you've seen my *book*.

Kittens love to play, play, play!
With some yarn, they play all day!

Have you seen this book?

This book is missing a page. My little sister ripped it out.
I don't have any other books with knights and princesses,
so I took a page from my sister's book and taped it in.
If you find a book with a new page taped in, you'll
know for sure that's my book.

The dragon flapped his wings, swooped down from the sky, drew his fiery breath, and got smoke in his eye.

Have you seen this book?

Remember how I said my book has the biggest dragon I've ever seen? Well, that big dragon had an accident. No, not that kind of accident—dragons are potty-trained. If you've seen a dragon that had an accident, you've seen my book.

The fiercest of dragons,
which no one could slay,
cried like a baby,
then flew far, far away.

Have you seen this book?

This book has a dragon crying like a baby. That reminded me of when I was a baby. So I added a picture of me as a baby to the book. If you see a picture of a really, really cute baby, you'll know for sure that's my book!

The knight and the princess, filled with joy and laughter, saved the Kingdom of Yore and lived happily ever after.

Have you seen this book?
Wait, you've seen this book?
Do you love this book?
Do you want to read this book
again and again?